Fatima
the Face-Painting Fairy

by Daisy Meadows

ORCHARD

www.rainbowmagic.co.uk

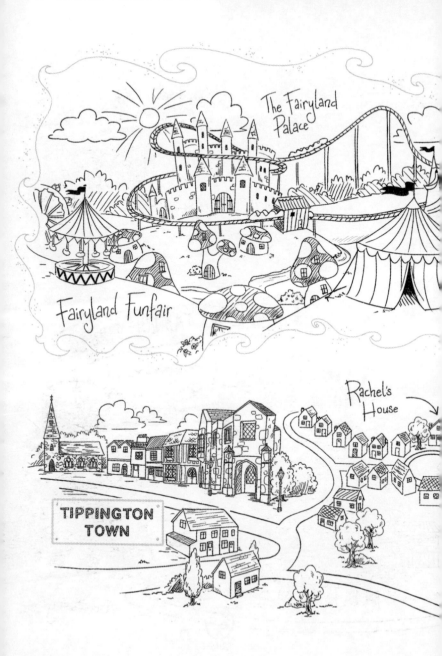

Fatima
the Face-Painting Fairy

the **Rainbow Magic Reading Challenge!**

story and collect your fairy points to climb the
ding Rainbow at the back of the book.

This book is worth 5 points.

To Poppy, with love

Special thanks to
Rachel Elliot

ORCHARD BOOKS

First published in Great Britain in 2018 by The Watts Publishing Group

1 3 5 7 9 10 8 6 4 2

© 2018 Rainbow Magic Limited.
© 2018 HIT Entertainment Limited.
Illustrations © Orchard Books 2018

HIT entertainment

A CIP catalogue record for this book is available from the British Library.

ISBN 978 1 40834 959 5

Printed and bound in Great Britain by CPI Group (UK) Ltd, Croydon, CR0 4YY

Orchard Books
An imprint of Hachette Children's Group
Part of The Watts Publishing Group Limited
Carmelite House, 50 Victoria Embankment, London EC4Y 0DZ

An Hachette UK Company
www.hachette.co.uk
www.hachettechildrens.co.uk

Jack Frost's Spell

I want a funfair just for me!
(I'll let in goblins, grudgingly.)
With stolen keyrings in my hand,
I'll spoil the fun the fairies planned.

Their rides will stop, their stalls will fail,
Their food will all turn sour and stale.
I'll make the goblins squeal and smirk.
This time my plan is going to work!

Contents

Silly Mirrors

Kirsty Tate popped the last, scrumptious bite of hot dog into her mouth and licked her fingers. Her best friend, Rachel Walker, had already finished her burger. She was pulling funny faces in the silly mirrors outside the funhouse.

"I love these," said Rachel, pulling her ears out so they looked huge and wobbly in the mirror. "I think they might be my favourite thing at the funfair."

"You've said that about everything so far," said Kirsty, giggling.

The girls were spending the day at The Fernandos' Fabulous Funfair. It had come to the playing field of Rachel's school in Tippington, and Kirsty was visiting for the weekend so that they could enjoy it together.

"The Zippy Zoom rollercoaster was lots of fun," said Kirsty, coming to stand beside Rachel in front of the first mirror.

"So was the Lucky Dip," said Rachel, moving on to the second mirror. "And it was great to make some new friends."

Matilda and Georgia Fernando were twin sisters whose parents ran the funfair. The girls had met them when they arrived, and they had got on instantly.

"I look hilarious," said Kirsty, staring at herself in the first mirror. "I'm just like a beanpole. "

She bent her knees and bobbed up and down, giggling as her reflection grew tall and bendy.

"Come and see this one," said Rachel, chuckling at herself looking as round as a beach ball, with a tiny head.

The girls laughed as they moved along the row of mirrors, changing shape in each one. But when they reached the last mirror, their reflections seemed normal.

"What's funny about this one?" said Rachel.

The girls stared at themselves, and then Kirsty saw it.

"Look at our feet," she said, bursting with laughter.

Their feet looked enormous, as if they were wearing clown shoes.

"That's brilliant," said Rachel, lifting one foot after the other and waggling them around.

But then Kirsty spotted something

in the mirror that made her forget all about her huge feet. Spinning around, she grabbed Rachel's arm and pointed at a boy walking through the crowd.

"Can you see what I see?" she asked her best friend. "Is that ... can that possibly be Jack Frost?"

Rachel gaped at the boy. He had a blue face and a beard that made him look exactly like the fairies' worst enemy.

"He can't be," said Rachel. "He's too short, and look at his feet – they're tiny."

Even so, he looked so like the Ice Lord that the girls could feel their legs shaking. Then, as the boy got closer, relief flooded through Kirsty.

"It's paint," she said. "It's just face paint. It must be a stick-on beard."

Rachel stepped out in front of the boy.

"Your face paint looks cool," she said. "What is it meant to be?"

The boy frowned, which made him

look even more like Jack Frost than ever.

"I asked to be a tiger," he said. "But the man at the face-painting stall gave me this. I don't know what it's supposed to be, but I don't like it."

He stomped off, and the girls exchanged a worried look.

"It seems Jack hasn't finished causing trouble here at the funfair," said Kirsty.

Just that morning, they had shared an amazing adventure with Rae the Rollercoaster Fairy. She had whisked them to Fairyland, where the Funfair Fairies were getting ready for the Summer Fair at the Fairyland Palace. Jack Frost and his goblins had stolen magical objects from Rae and the rest of the Funfair Fairies – Fatima the Face-Painting Fairy, Paloma the Dodgems Fairy and Bobbi the Bouncy Castle Fairy. Back at the funfair, Rachel and Kirsty had found Jack Frost's goblins riding the Zippy Zoom rollercoaster, and they had managed to get Rae's key ring back.

"Jack Frost still has three of the key rings," said Rachel. "Without them, the fairies can't make sure that all funfairs are as fun as can be."

Queen Titania
and King
Oberon had
asked Rachel
and Kirsty to
help the fairies
get their key rings
back. Until the key

rings were back with their
rightful owners, there would be trouble
at the Fairyland Summer Fair and at
funfairs everywhere, including the one in
Tippington.

"Everyone's depending on us to stop
Jack Frost," said Kirsty. "We've already
helped Rae find her key ring. We can
find the other three."

Fatima Appears

mirrors, and then gasped. A magical glow was coming from the top of the big-foot mirror.

"Look, Kirsty," she whispered.

The girls leaned forward to have a closer look, and the light grew brighter. Then they saw the tips of two delicate wings, and a tiny pair of eyes peeped at them over the top of the mirror. It was

Fatima the Face-Painting Fairy. Feeling excited, Rachel and Kirsty hurried around to the hidden space behind the double-sided mirrors. The little fairy was waiting for them there.

Fatima was wearing a jumpsuit as dark

blue as the night sky, and sprinkled with golden stars. Her sandals were golden too, and her long overshirt glimmered with flecks of silver thread. Even her wings were tinged with gold.

"Fatima!" cried Kirsty. "I'm so

glad you're here. Something is wrong
with the funfair's face-painter. We've just
seen a boy who was painted to look
exactly like Jack Frost."

Fatima nodded, combing her fingers
through her tousled brown hair.

"Jack Frost has still got my magical
mirror key ring," she said. "Without it,

face-painting all over the human and fairy worlds is going wrong. There's nothing I can do to put it right."

"We're ready to help you get your key ring back," said Rachel at once. "We were able to help Rae find hers, and the more of us there are searching for it, the better chance we have of finding it."

"Thank you," said Fatima, giving them a wide, warm smile. "I just don't know where to start looking."

"Let's begin at the face-painting stall," said Kirsty. "It sounds as if something strange is going on there."

Fatima darted into Rachel's pocket and the girls hurried off, looking for the face-painting stall.

"It must be this way," said Rachel, pointing along the path between the

dodgems and the Ferris wheel.
"That boy was coming from this
direction."

Walking quickly, the girls weaved their

way among the slow-moving crowds.
Their eyes skimmed over the colourful,
noisy stalls offering games, food and
rides. The school playing field was
ringing with laughter and happy voices,
but Rachel and Kirsty could think only
about Jack Frost, and what he was doing
to face-painting all over the world.

"Look up ahead," said Kirsty, pointing
at two blonde girls in the bustling crowd.
"Isn't that Matilda and Georgia?

The girls quickened their pace, almost
running now. They reached out to touch
their new friends, and the sisters turned
around. Shocked, Rachel and Kirsty took
a step backwards.

Both girls looked just like Jack Frost!

"Don't say anything," Matilda said
with a groan. "We know our face paint

looks awful. Can you believe it? I asked to be a flower, and Georgia wanted to be a butterfly. So how come we ended up with blue faces and spiky beards?"

"It's the worst face paint I've ever had," said Georgia. "I don't know why our parents hired the new face-painter. Patrice has always done the funfair's face-painting, and she is brilliant. I can't

understand it."

Kirsty and Rachel exchanged a worried glance. A new face-painter? Things were quickly getting worse.

"Where is the face-painting stall?" Rachel asked.

"Oh my goodness, you're not going to get your faces painted, are you?" Matilda asked.

"We just want to see everything at the funfair," said Kirsty.

"I'm not sure this is worth seeing," said Georgia with a rueful laugh. "I think the new face-painter is only interested in painting one style."

"He's over there," said Matilda, pointing across the playing field.

"Why don't you come with us?" said Rachel. "You could ask for your money

back."

"We already tried that," said Georgia with a sigh. "He said no. We're going to see our parents now. Maybe they'll be able to stop this new face-painter. See you later."

The sisters hurried away, and Rachel and Kirsty turned to walk towards the face-painting stall.

"Matilda and Georgia's parents won't be able to put this right," said Kirsty.

"It's a magical problem, and it needs a magical solution."

Too Many Jacks

The girls made their way across the
playing field, passing more and more
people painted to look like Jack Frost.
Blue faces and spiky beards seemed to be
everywhere, and the girls went faster and
faster until they were running. They only
stopped when they got to the large face-
painting stall.

"Is Jack Frost there?" asked Fatima.

"No," said Kirsty. "The only person I can see is a lady."

The lady was standing behind a sign that said 'Faces Painted by Patrice'.

"She must be Patrice, the face-painter who Georgia mentioned," said Rachel. "She looks nice. Let's go and ask her if she knows about the blue faces."

They went up to the stall.

"Hello, are you Patrice?" Kirsty asked.

The lady gave them a kind smile.

"Yes I am," she said. "But I'm sorry, dears. My face paints have dried up, and I can't use a single one of them. They're rock hard. I might as well pack up and go home."

"We've seen a lot of people with blue faces and beards," said Rachel. "Do you know who painted them?"

"I do," said Patrice, giving a sigh. "If that's the kind of face paint you want, it's over there."

She pointed to the edge of the field, which was lined with oak trees.

"Let's go and investigate," said Kirsty.

Below the trees was a little face-painting stall. A blue sign arched over a table, with the words 'WANT TO LOOK ACE? LET ME PAINT YOUR FACE' printed in glittering silver letters. Blue cardboard icicles dangled from the sign. A long queue of children was winding away from the face-painting table, and they were all chattering and smiling. But the children who were walking away from the table were looking glum. Every single one of them had a face painted like Jack Frost, with a stick-on beard to complete the look.

"I asked to look like a superhero," one

boy grumbled. "But now I look more like a super villain."

"This beard is really tickly," a little girl wailed.

Rachel and Kirsty shared a worried look.

"Jack Frost is so vain," Rachel said.

"He's painting everyone's faces to look just like him."

The man sitting at the face-painting table had a blue face and a long, spiky beard. He looked exactly like Jack Frost. But so did all the other people who were walking around the table.

"How can we be sure that's the real Jack Frost, and not a goblin in disguise?" Kirsty asked in a low voice.

She stared at him, trying to figure out a way to tell who he was. Then she saw his feet. They were poking out from under the table, and they were not as large as goblins' feet. Instead, they were in blue, glittery boots that curled up at the toes.

"It *is* him," she said, nudging Rachel. "Look at his feet. No one else wears boots like that."

"I didn't know he was so artistic," said Rachel. "I know it's awful that he's painting everyone the same, but it's amazing how realistic the faces are."

"It's because he has my magical mirror key ring with him," said Fatima, peeping out of Rachel's bag. "My magic is helping him to do face-painting really well."

"It's wonderful that we've found it," said Rachel. "Now we need a way to get it back, and I've got an idea."

Rachel whispered her idea to Kirsty

and Fatima. Then the girls joined the long queue. They stood and listened to the other children chattering about how they wanted their faces painted. They heard people wishing for dragons, ice queens, frogs, fairies and butterflies. It made the girls feel awful to imagine how disappointed all these children were going to be.

"We have to stop Jack Frost from spoiling everyone's day," said Kirsty under her breath.

The queue was long, but at last it was their turn. Trembling a little, they stepped forwards.

Painted by Jack Frost

Kirsty sat down in front of Jack Frost.

"Hi, I'd like to be a dragonfly," she said.

"You'll get what you're given,"
Jack Frost growled.

He leaned forwards and started
to paint her face. Kirsty tried hard not to
shiver. It made her feel nervous to be this
close to the Ice Lord. She could feel his

breath on her face, and she hoped that
his sharp, beady eyes wouldn't recognise
her.

Rachel watched Jack Frost dab blue
paint on to Kirsty's face. He was doing
an expert job, and Rachel felt quite cross
about how he was misusing Fatima's
face-painting magic.

"I don't think that's the right shade of blue," she said. "It's not the same wishy-washy blue as your face."

"Rubbish," said Jack Frost. "It's exactly the same. And my face isn't wishy-washy."

He used black paint to give Kirsty angry eyebrows and frown wrinkles. Then he stuck the beard on to her chin. Rachel shook her head.

"That beard doesn't look like yours," she said. "Hers is spiky and yours is more fluffy. Like a lovely, fluffy, white kitten."

Jack Frost made

an outraged spluttering noise.

"My beard looks nothing like a fluffy kitten," he snapped. "Stop saying that. It's perfect, and so is my face-painting work. I'm an artist."

"Sorry, but you're making a mistake," said Rachel. "I'm looking at both of you and it's definitely not the same. You should look in the mirror."

Jack Frost scowled and grumbled, but he reached into his pocket and pulled out a round, golden key ring. He pressed a tiny button, the lid flew open, and a

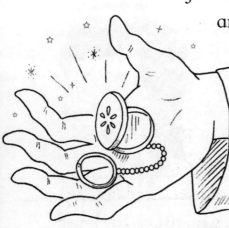

mirror sparkled in the sunshine.

"Look at me, I'm gorgeous," he said, preening himself in the mirror.

WHOOSH! As quick as a flash,

Fatima swooped out of Rachel's bag and zoomed towards her key ring. No one in the queue could see her because the girls were in the way. But Jack Frost glimpsed her out of the corner of his eye.

He sprang to his feet and his chair flew backwards.

"Oh no, you don't," he hissed. "You silly fairies can't get the better of me."

Kirsty jumped up too, and Rachel

glanced back at the other children in the queue. Everyone was staring in surprise.

"Give Fatima her key ring," Kirsty said in a quiet voice. "We won't let you get away with this."

Jack Frost threw back his head and laughed.

"I already have got away with it," he said. "Tough luck, Fatima."

Clutching the magical mirror key ring, he sprinted away from the stall. The children in the queue groaned, and Rachel and Kirsty looked at each other in alarm.

"How are we going to get the key ring

back?" Kirsty asked.

"Hide behind the stall," said Fatima, slipping back into Rachel's pocket.

The girls darted out of sight. As the queue of children started to break up and people wandered away, Fatima fluttered out of the pocket and lifted her wand up.

"Is it OK if I turn you into fairies?" she asked. "We'll be able to follow Jack Frost more easily if we can all fly."

Rachel and Kirsty nodded at once. It was always exciting to be turned into fairies. Fatima smiled and spoke the words of a spell:

"Faster than a fairy's blink,
Dwindle down and quickly shrink.
Flutter, wings, as light as air,
And follow Jack Frost everywhere!"

At once, a shower of golden stars fell

down on the girls, catching in their hair
and on their eyelashes. They felt the
delicious tickle of magic on their skin,
and then they shrank to fairy size, their
wings lifting them upwards.

"I love this feeling," said Rachel,

twirling as she flew higher. "It's always so dizzying and exciting, no matter how many times we do it."

The three fairies swooped high over the funfair. From there, they could see people with blue painted faces dotted all through the crowd.

"Which one is Jack Frost?" Fatima asked. "How can we tell?"

Kirsty remembered seeing Jack Frost's glittering blue boots poking out from

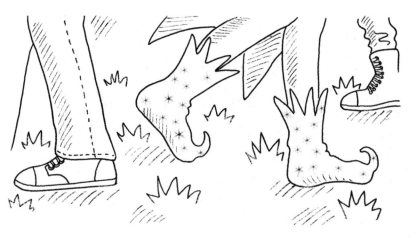

under the face-painting table.

"We have to look for his feet," she said.

She dived downwards with Rachel and Fatima, flying so low that their stomachs brushed against the grass. They weaved in and out of a forest of legs. Big feet, small feet, wide feet and narrow feet stomped around them. None of them belonged to Jack Frost. Then Rachel saw a pair of glittering blue boots with curly toes. The boots were running, and people were scurrying out of the way.

"I'd know those boots anywhere," Rachel cried. "That's him!"

Blue and Beautiful

The fairies chased Jack Frost through the crowd, dodging around the legs of adults, children and dogs.

"He's heading towards the funhouse," called Rachel over her shoulder.

"Let's try to corner him at the silly mirrors," said Kirsty. "He's so vain that he's sure to slow down when he sees them. He won't be able to resist taking a look at himself."

Just then, Jack Frost changed direction, running too far to the left.

"Oh no," cried Fatima. "He's going to miss the mirrors."

"I've got an idea," said Kirsty.

She put on a burst of speed and tickled his ankles. Rachel joined in, and Jack Frost squeaked and leaped into the air. Then he veered to the right.

"Yes!" said Kirsty. "He's heading straight towards the mirrors."

"He's slowing down," said Fatima.

Sure enough, Jack Frost couldn't resist stopping in front of the first mirror to gaze at his reflection.

"No!" he cried. "I don't look like that."

He bobbed up and down, trying to make his reflection look normal. But everything he did made him look more peculiar.

"I'm not that skinny," he muttered, moving on to the next mirror. "There's something wrong with that one."

The next mirror made him appear short and squat.

"I look like a frog," he raged. "What's the matter with this thing?"

He bent down and peered at himself upside down. It didn't help. The next mirror was the one that made him look as round as a beach ball, with a tiny head. Seething, he snatched the mirror key ring out of his pocket and clicked it open.

"Just as I thought," he exclaimed. "In this mirror I look just as handsome as

ever. Perhaps even more so."

He held the mirror up high, looking up into it with sunlight shining on his face.

"Ah, what a gorgeous sight," he said, preening himself. "Blue and beautiful."

Just then, the sun shone in his eyes. For a second, he squeezed them shut. Rachel and Kirsty seized the moment. They rocketed upwards and swiped the key ring from Jack Frost's hand in one smooth movement.

"Hey, give that back!" he yelled,
jumping up and snatching at them in the
air.

The best friends zigzagged out of his
way, and felt the key ring slipping out of
their tiny fingers.

"It's too heavy," cried Rachel.

She and Kirsty fluttered their wings as

hard as they could, but they were sinking down towards Jack Frost's grasping hands. Then Fatima zoomed up to Rachel and Kirsty, and as soon as she touched the key ring, it shrank to fairy size. The fairies darted out of sight behind the mirrors, and Jack Frost stomped after them.

"Give it to me, you annoying little pests," he demanded.

"It's not yours," said Rachel.

"Why do you want it?" Fatima asked.

"I want to make everyone look like me," he said, snarling at them. "I'm tired of looking around and seeing stupid fairy faces and gormless goblin faces. There's only one face that I'll never get tired of seeing. Mine!"

"But you're special," said Kirsty. "You're

one of a kind. There's no one else in the human or fairy worlds like you. Why would you want everyone else to look the same as you?"

Jack Frost glared at her with suspicion in his eyes.

"Why are you saying that?" he demanded. "It's all true, of course, but what would make you suddenly start talking sense?"

Just then, he heard a giggle. Rachel was

hovering beside the middle mirror, laughing. The mirrors were double-sided, so she could see her funny reflection even though they were behind it.

"What are you doing?" Jack Frost shouted. "Those stupid mirrors don't even work."

"You're wrong," Rachel said, with another burst of laughter. "They're wonderful. Just look at me."

She pointed at her reflection, and Kirsty giggled when she saw Rachel's little fairy body with great big feet waggling around underneath it. Kirsty fluttered forward and spluttered with laughter when she saw herself in the mirror. Her fairy body looked as round as a berry, and her head was so small that it had almost disappeared.

Rachel, Kirsty and Fatima couldn't help themselves. Bubbling with relief that they had got the key ring back, they felt full of fun. Jack Frost's frown grew deeper and deeper as he watched them pulling faces in the silly mirrors, holding on to

each other and helpless
with laughter.

"Stop
laughing,"
he hissed
through his
teeth. "Give
me that
key ring. Be
quiet."

He stamped his
foot. He roared and
shouted. But the fairies just laughed more
and more.

"We can't help it," said Kirsty, wiping
tears of laughter from her eyes. "It's just
so funny."

"You're a pack of fools," Jack Frost
yelled. "I'm going home."

There was a bolt of icy blue magic, and the Ice Lord vanished back to his castle.

Painted by Patrice

Still laughing, the fairies peeped out from behind the silly mirrors. There were lots of people passing by and laughing as they glanced at their own reflections. But no one could see the fairies.

Fatima threw her arms around Rachel and Kirsty and they all shared a hug.

"You have both been amazing,"

she said. "You're so kind to help me. I wouldn't have been able to get my key ring back all by myself."

"We want to help all the Funfair Fairies," said Kirsty. "It's not fair that Jack Frost should get away with his naughty plans."

"Queen Titania and King Oberon will be happy to hear that another of the key rings is back where it belongs," said Fatima. "I can't wait to tell them. But first …"

She waved her wand and the girls grew to human size again. Their fairy wings disappeared.

"Thanks to you, the face-painting at funfairs everywhere will make children happy again," said Fatima, hovering between them. "Now I can go back to

the Summer Fair in Fairyland with good news."

"Goodbye," said Rachel.

"It was lovely to get to know you," Kirsty added.

Fatima waved her wand around herself, creating a circle of golden fairy dust that wound around her like a ribbon. The circle grew smaller and then disappeared, taking Fatima with it.

Rachel and Kirsty stepped out from behind the funny mirrors and smiled at each other.

"What would you like to do now?" Rachel asked.

"Let's get our faces painted," said Kirsty.

"It'll be fun, and a really good way to check that everything is back to normal."

"Great plan," said Rachel. "And I know exactly what we should ask for. Fairy faces!"

Side by side, they ran back to the place where the face-painting stalls were set up. Jack Frost's stall had vanished, but Patrice was still there. She had packed up her paints and was just about to fold up her face-painting table.

"Hello again, girls," she said. "I'm just about to head home. Are you looking for the blue-faced painter?"

"No," said Kirsty. "We're looking for you!"

"We want to have fairy faces," said Rachel. "Please will you do it for us? Matilda and Georgia said you're an amazing face-painter."

"I wish I could," said Patrice. "Don't you remember what I told you? All my face paints have dried up."

"Could you check them again?" Kirsty asked, clasping her hands together in a pleading way. "Please, Patrice?"

Patrice looked at her for a moment and then picked up a large, black case and put it on the table.

"I'll show you," she said. "My poor
paints are ruined."

She opened the case with a click, and
lifted the lid. Rachel and Kirsty saw
her expression change from sadness to
surprise. Her eyes widened, and then
she looked up at
the girls with her
mouth open.

"I can hardly
believe it," she said.
"My paints are
absolutely fine.
How could this
have happened? It's
almost like magic."

She laughed, and
Kirsty and Rachel
exchanged a secret

smile. They couldn't tell Patrice the truth because they had promised to keep the fairies a secret. But they knew that the world was full of magic.

Rachel sat down on the chair and Patrice got her paints ready. Just then, Kirsty spotted Matilda and Georgia walking past. Their faces were clean again, and they were smiling.

"Matilda, Georgia!" Kirsty called. "We're getting our faces painted. Patrice's paints are back to normal."

The sisters came skipping over to them, looking excited.

"That's brilliant," said Georgia. "We've just seen that the other stall has gone."

Rachel and Kirsty shared a happy smile.

"You should get your faces done again,

too," said Rachel.

Matilda and Georgia agreed at once, and they all crowded around to watch Patrice paint Rachel's face. Shortly a queue of people had formed, excited to have their faces painted how they chose.

Patrice worked fast, and Rachel and
Kirsty soon had sparkly fairy faces.
Matilda chose to be a tropical flower, and
Georgia became a butterfly.

"You all look amazing," said Rachel,
smiling at Kirsty, Matilda and Georgia.

"I told you Patrice is the best," said
Matilda.

Rachel glanced at her watch and sighed.

"It's time for us to say goodbye," she said. "We have to go home for tea."

"Will you come back again tomorrow?" Georgia asked. "There's still a lot more fun to have here."

Rachel and Kirsty exchanged a worried glance. They knew that no one would be having fun if the Funfair Fairies couldn't get all their key rings back.

"Of course we will," said Kirsty.

They all hugged, and then Rachel and Kirsty set off for Rachel's house. They walked out under the big sign that said, 'The Fernandos' Fabulous Funfair'.

"It *is* a fabulous funfair," said Rachel, glancing up at the sign. "I hope we can find the other two magical key

rings soon, or funfairs everywhere will
stop being fabulous. I know Jack Frost
will carry on trying to spoil things for
everyone."

The best friends linked arms and Kirsty
smiled at Rachel.

"We will find the other two key rings,"

she said. "The Fairyland Summer Fair opens tomorrow night, and the fairies are depending on us. We will never let them down!"

The End

Now it's time for Kirsty and
Rachel to help...

Paloma the Dodgems Fairy

Read on for a sneak peek...

"I wish The Fernandos' Fabulous Funfair
could stay on my school playing field for
ever," said Rachel Walker as she skipped
along. "I had a brilliant time yesterday,
and there's still so much more to do."

"Can you imagine having a funfair at
school?" said her best friend, Kirsty Tate.
"No one would get any lessons done."

"And we wouldn't want to leave at
home time," Rachel added with a giggle.

The sun was shining, and the girls were
looking forward to another exciting
day at the funfair. Kirsty was staying
with Rachel all weekend, and they

were planning to spend every possible moment enjoying the funfair. Up ahead, they could see two girls leaning over the wooden entrance gate and waving at them.

"Morning, Matilda!" called Rachel. "Hi, Georgia!"

Matilda and Georgia Fernando were twin sisters, and their parents ran the funfair. Rachel and Kirsty had met them the day before, and the four girls had made friends straight away.

"Good morning," said Matilda, grinning at them. "I'm glad you're here so early – we've got so much to show you! What do you want to try first?"

"What would you choose?" Kirsty asked.

"How about the dodgems?" said Georgia, her eyes sparkling. "They're always fun."

"Oh yes, I love dodgems," said Rachel.

They bought their tickets from the little booth that stood just inside the gate. Today, the tickets were ruby red with a rainbow-coloured trim.

"These tickets are even more beautiful than yesterday's purple ones," said Kirsty.

"We sell a different coloured ticket every day," said Matilda. "We go through all the colours of the rainbow."

Rachel and Kirsty exchanged a secret smile as they all ran into the playing field. Talking of rainbows always reminded them of the first fairies they had ever met, the Rainbow Fairies. Since then they had shared many adventures with the fairies.

"This way to the dodgems," called Matilda.

She and her sister led Rachel and Kirsty over to the red-and-gold dodgem rink. Coloured lights were flashing and summery songs were blasting out. Even though it was early, there were already a few children in the cars.

The operator was a young woman with short brown hair.

"Hi, Becky," called Matilda, waving to her.

Read **Paloma the Dodgems Fairy** to find out what adventures are in store for Kirsty and Rachel!

Calling all parents, carers and teachers!
The Rainbow Magic fairies are here to help
your child enter the magical world of reading.
Whatever reading stage they are at, there's
a Rainbow Magic book for everyone!
Here is Lydia the Reading Fairy's guide to
supporting your child's journey at all levels.

Starting Out

1 Our Rainbow Magic Beginner Readers are perfect for first-time readers who are just beginning to develop reading skills and confidence. Approved by teachers, they contain a full range of educational levelling, as well as lively full-colour illustrations.

Developing Readers

2 Rainbow Magic Early Readers contain longer stories and wider vocabulary for building stamina and growing confidence. These are adaptations of our most popular Rainbow Magic stories, specially developed for younger readers in conjunction with an Early Years reading consultant, with full-colour illustrations.

Going Solo

3 The Rainbow Magic chapter books – a mixture of series and one-off specials – contain accessible writing to encourage your child to venture into reading independently. These highly collectible and much-loved magical stories inspire a love of reading to last a lifetime.

www.rainbowmagicbooks.co.uk

"Rainbow Magic got my daughter reading chapter books. Great sparkly covers, cute fairies and traditional stories full of magic that she found impossible to put down" - Mother of Edie (6 years)

"Florence LOVES the Rainbow Magic books. She really enjoys reading now" - Mother of Florence (6 years)

The Rainbow Magic Reading Challenge

Well done, fairy friend – you have completed the book!
This book was worth 5 points.

See how far you have climbed on the
Reading Rainbow opposite.

The more books you read, the more points you will get,
and the closer you will be to becoming a Fairy Princess!

How to get your Reading Rainbow
1. Cut out the coin below
2. Go to the Rainbow Magic website
3. Download and print out your poster
4. Add your coin and climb up the Reading Rainbow!

There's all this and lots more at
www.rainbowmagicbooks.co.uk

You'll find activities, competitions, stories, a special
newsletter and complete profiles of all the
Rainbow Magic fairies. Find a fairy with your name!